THE
CITY
GIRLS

THE CITY GIRLS

Aki

GODWINBOOKS

Henry Holt and Company

New York

Laura

Miffy

Annie

Rebecca

Jane

Vanessa

June

Melanie

It's morning time in the city.
We watch the sun rise, slow and pretty.

NICE

Baked-bread smells and coffee carts.
Doors roll up at super-marts.

Busy men and women, riding.
Busy kids with parents, guiding.

Everyone is crossing streets—
Lights and whistles,
honks and tweets!

Uh-oh! We feel drops of rain.

Down we go · We'll take the train.

Minutes later, here's our stop.
It's our favorite bookshop!

At the museum, we show our passes.
We take a tour and wave at classes.

Everyone's hungry. We file inside.
Eggs over easy, poached,
and fried!

The park is filled with flowers.
Around its edges stand tall towers.

The sun is setting.
We leave the park.
We must get home
before it's dark!

Taxis race us side by side.
We thank our driver for the ride.

Back upstairs, it's such a sight . . .
Bright lights on a city night.

MORE TO EXPLORE!
LIFE INSIDE AND OUTSIDE THE CITY

Communities of people form in all different environments.

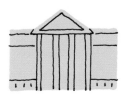 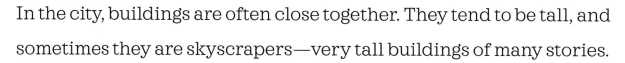 BUILDINGS AND STRUCTURES

In the city, buildings are often close together. They tend to be tall, and sometimes they are skyscrapers—very tall buildings of many stories.

In the suburbs, buildings are often more spread out. They tend to be shorter.

In the country, buildings are often far apart. Whether farmland, woodland, plains, or deserts, there tends to be more open land without buildings.

 PLANT LIFE

In the city, there are often few plants. They tend to be in parks or other green areas.

In the suburbs, there are more plants. Grass lawns and trees can be big or small.

In the country, there are often lots of plants. Nature is everywhere!

HOUSING AND HOMES

In the city, people often live close together in apartments. There tend to be many separate homes in one building.

In the suburbs, people often live in houses or apartments in neighborhoods.

In the country, people often live in houses farther apart from one another.

TRANSPORTATION

In the city, there is often public transportation—buses or subways that help people get around. People also walk and bicycle between places.

In the suburbs, there is sometimes public transportation like buses. Often, people drive cars or personal vehicles.

In the country, it is more common for people to drive cars or personal vehicles.

Henry Holt and Company

Publishers since 1866

Henry Holt® is a registered trademark of Macmillan Publishing Group, LLC

120 Broadway, New York, NY 10271 • mackids.com

Library of Congress Control Number : 2019940920

ISBN 978-1-250-31395-9

Our books may be purchased in bulk for promotional, educational, or business use.
Please contact your local bookseller or the Macmillan Corporate and Premium
Sales Department at (800) 221-7945 ext. 5442 or by email at MacmillanSpecialMarkets@macmillan.com.

First edition, 2020 / Designed by April Ward

Printed in China by RR Donnelley Asia Printing Solutions Ltd., Dongguan City, Guangdong Province

1 3 5 7 9 10 8 6 4 2